Personal Best **2**

All That Jazz

ELIZABETH HUTCHINS

Illustrated by Michelle Ker

A Haights Cross Communications Company

Published by
Sundance Publishing
P.O. Box 1326
234 Taylor Street
Littleton, MA 01460
800-343-8204

Copyright © text Elizabeth Hutchins 2001
Copyright © illustrations Michelle Ker 2001

First published 2001 as Supa Dazzlers by
Pearson Education Australia Pty Limited
95 Coventry Street
South Melbourne 3205 Australia
Exclusive United States Distribution: Sundance Publishing

ISBN 0-7608-6176-5

Printed in Canada

Contents

Chapter 1

Battle
Lines

"A little bit of you, makes me your m . . . !"

A huge thump made the CD player miss two beats. That bumped me back into the real world. There was my stepbrother Tony. He was leaping across the family room with his arms stretched wide.

Tony was screeching above my song as he imitated my dance steps. And he had one of my ballet tutus stretched around his waist!

"GET LOST, Tony! Do you have to ruin everything I do?"

I made a face at Tony, as I thought about the cast on my wrist. It was the wrist he'd broken last month when we were skiing. When he saw my face, he patted my head and said, "You keep playing your little games." Then he tiptoed out of the room pretending to be a ballet dancer.

Little games! I was boiling inside.

The best, the *very* best thing about my life is jazz ballet. And the best part of jazz ballet is the music. I couldn't live without my head filled with all of those great tunes. Sometimes I sing along while I make up new dance routines. Then I try them out on Mom. At least, that's how it used to be. That was before Tony and his brother Owen came to live with us.

Even though I have problems with Tony, he's the least of my worries. At the top of my list is Rick, my new stepfather. If he had his way, I wouldn't be dancing at all.

When he got the bill for my lessons, he freaked out. Then he called one of his many family meetings. "We can't afford extras like Mel's dancing lessons," he said. "She can take up basketball at school."

"Basketball?" I exclaimed. "I don't like basketball. It's silly to run the length of the court with the ball and . . ."

"Try soccer, then," grinned Tony.

"Team sports teach you to work with other people," Rick said.

I nearly choked. Didn't Rick know how closely you have to work with the other dancers?

Mom began, "Mel's been taking ballet since she was four, and . . ." But Rick interrupted.

"Does she have to belong to *three* classes?" he asked.

I explained that I have my Saturday classes. Then I have to do an hour of classical ballet to keep up my basic skills. And I also have a private lesson with Miss Narelle. That's when I learn new steps.

"She's not giving up dancing," said Mom firmly.

She and Rick glared at each other for a minute. But we won this round. I could keep up my classes—for now. I knew we hadn't heard the last of this, though. The battle lines were drawn.

Chapter 2

More
Problems

With Rick and Tony against me, and a broken wrist, you'd think I had enough problems. But it got worse. On my first Saturday back after missing four weeks of lessons, I was in for a shock.

When I got to class, a new girl was stretching at the bar. She was smiling at herself in the long mirror in the hall. She was not just *any* new girl. She was even taller than me. And she was very graceful. Her black hair was tied up with a silk band. She wore a powder-blue leotard that matched her eyes.

She ignored us all as we chatted. Then Miss Narelle came in and said, "All right, everyone, in your lines! Pam, are you planning to join us?"

Pam. At the time I didn't know just how sick I'd get of hearing that name.

Pam was in the middle of the front row in the Egyptian dance. Everyone had been learning it while I was out. That was usually *my* spot. OK, so I was jealous.

I got stuck in the back row. From there, I could watch the moves and not be seen. Fair enough. It's hard to look graceful with your arm in a cast.

I found myself next to another fairly new girl, Beth. She was having real trouble with the steps. When she moved the wrong way, I hit her with my cast.

"Sorry!" I said. She rubbed her hand, but
looked at me in a friendly way.

A little later, Pam told Beth, "Watch it, stupid!" I motioned Beth over to one side, and we tried out the new steps together.

When there was a break, Beth asked me about my arm. I told her how Tony had smashed into me with his snowboard. "Another month of this awful cast," I said. (I'd explained what happened so often that I should have had a sign made!)

Everyone was listening by now. Miss Narelle said, "Well, that's too bad, because the competition is in four weeks. I guess you won't enter it now."

My heart sank to my ballet shoes. The Dance Society's competition is the highlight of the year, apart from the winter recital. It was my second year at this age level, so I'd been hoping to do really well.

One of the boys, Matthew, said he'd wanted to do a duet with me. He's a super dancer—as well as being drop-dead gorgeous. So I was already feeling really miserable when Pam stepped up to Matthew. "Can I take Mel's place?" she asked. "I'm sure we'll make a great couple." She smiled sweetly at him, and something exploded inside my brain!

"I've decided to enter anyway," I announced.

I'd show everyone! Too bad about my cast. My broken hand might lose me points. I'd just have to make them up with great timing and footwork.

Chapter 3

Pam
the
Enemy

During my lesson on Thursday, Miss Narelle taught me the rest of the new dance. She was pleased that I was able to learn it so quickly.

The dance really did look Egyptian. We had to do snake arms and jerk our necks forward. Then we stomped with our feet and knees in and then out.

Miss Narelle is really agile and limber. She can even put her leg behind her neck! She is such fun to be around. I just love working with her!

On Saturday, the whole class met. Miss Narelle had us work on the Egyptian dance. She explained that the dance would start with all of us behind each other in a single line. The audience would see a single body (Pam's, of course) and 16 waving arms. Then, one-by-one, we would leap out from behind Pam.

I wanted to go to the left, so that I could point my good arm. But that would mess up the order. "Perhaps someone will change with me," I said. And I turned and looked right at Pam.

Miss Narelle shook her head and looked slightly amused. She said, "I'm sorry, Mel, but Pam is going to stay where she is for now. She's very talented, you know." So that left me behind Beth. And that was at the very back of the line.

Next we worked out the music for my solos. Everyone chooses their own music. I had six routines worked out. We added two that Miss Narelle had ready. But the one I really wanted to do was *Opposites Attract* with Matthew.

Miss Narelle suddenly looked at the clock. She said, "See if the others are here for your trio, Mel."

Trio? Puzzled, I went to open the door. There were Pam and Beth. Just by looking at their faces, it was easy to see that they weren't getting along.

"All right!" said Miss Narelle. "We've got ten minutes. Beth, it will be good for you to learn a dance with two of my star pupils." Beth looked unsure, and Pam's face flashed with anger.

Didn't Miss Narelle pick up all of the bad vibes? Surely there had never been a less united trio than this one! Poor Beth got more confused as Pam sighed and glared at her. The tension started to get to me. What a waste of time! At the end, even Miss Narelle picked on Beth. She said that she'd have to work hard to stop sickling her feet.

Pam stormed off to her ballet class. And Beth, nearly in tears, said, "I don't even know what sickling is." I told her it's when your foot bends over backward and curves like a sickle.

I'm usually slow to make friends, but Beth looked sad. So I found myself saying, "Why don't you come to my house one day to practice?"

Of course she was thrilled. She introduced me to her mother on the way out. We arranged for Beth to come over for lunch on Saturday.

I'd have to make sure that Tony behaved.

Chapter 4

A
Bombshell

To my surprise, Tony promised not to bother us.

"Sure. Not a problem, Sis," he agreed, with a sugary smile.

So on Saturday, when Beth arrived, I greeted her cheerfully.

We got right down to some exercises. I had an idea that Beth needed to strengthen her legs. You see, if your thigh muscles aren't strong, that affects your knees and ankles. Then your toes buckle.

So I showed Beth some pre-ski exercises. Then Beth stood on tiptoes while leaning on the wall with her hands. Then she took away the support and stood without wobbling. "It feels better already," she said. "I'll try that every day."

It was all too good to last, of course. We were just doing some steps—one, two, three, *kick*—when Tony yelled, "Hey, kick this!" And then a football slammed into my stomach.

"You *promised*, Tony," I gasped. "Get out!"

Tony smirked. "But *you* know that promises don't mean anything, don't you, Sister? After all, you broke yours up at the ski lodge. So now we're even, aren't we?"

I won't tell you my reply. I'll just say that it wasn't very polite!

Mom separated us and sent Tony on his way. As she left, she said, "Mel, I'm too tired to cope with your fighting. I'm really sorry that you and Tony have a problem with each other. But you'll have to learn to get along with him."

I was surprised. What was wrong with Mom? I'd never heard her say that she couldn't cope with something. And she *never* complained about being tired.

Beth and I had a great time. We even let Owen join in after lunch. He had such good rhythm that I told him that he should take up jazz.

Then we tried on all of my costumes and planned to swap a few of them for the competition. Beth looked great in my Spanish dress!

When Beth's mother came to pick her up, we discussed costumes again. Mom turned pale when I said I needed eight different outfits for the competition. Then I told her that I needed more for the winter recital. "Oh dear," she said, "I don't know how I'm going to make any this year."

"What's wrong? You always make them," I said. That's when I found out why Mom was feeling so tired.

She hesitated, then dropped her bombshell. "I was going to tell you soon," she said. "Rick and I are having a baby."

Chapter 5

Rivalry

I got over the huge shock of Mom's news. And I decided that it would be nice to have a baby in the house. (As long as it didn't look like Tony!) Even Rick had a huge grin on his face. But he was not going to budge on one matter.

"You're *definitely* not to make Mel any new costumes," he told Mom.

"No problem. We'll get a dressmaker to do them," I said. At that, Rick exploded. Didn't I know that he wasn't made of money?

"We'll work something out," said Mom. But she looked worried.

That night, I had a nightmare. I was in the front row of the *Egyptian* dance in my *Spanish* dress. I woke up sweating.

At least in my dreams I made the front row. In class, I was still placed way at the back. When everyone came on stage doing cartwheels, I just had to stand around. But my problem only made my rivalry with Pam grow worse. One day I'd show her who was the best!

Pam never seemed to make a wrong dance move. But when Miss Narelle wasn't looking, she was quick to step on my toes. Or to give poor Beth a confusing lead. Or to stick up her nose in the air at the rest of us. Even the boys, who had been drooling over her at first, were ignoring Pam now.

Miss Narelle didn't seem to notice anything. Finally she announced, "Pam and Mel, I can't choose between the two of you. You're both great dancers. So this is what I've decided about the lead role in the finale for the winter recital. It will go to the one who does better in the Dance Society's competition next week."

Somehow I managed to keep calm until I reached Mom's car. Then I banged my cast against the dashboard and yelled, "It's not fair!"

"What's not fair?" Mom asked. When I told her, she looked thoughtful. She asked when the competition was. When we got home, she headed for the phone.

I was alarmed. "I'll be *so* embarrassed if you phone Miss Narelle!" I said. She waved me off to my bedroom.

Three minutes later she came in, looking pleased with herself. "Now you can compete with Pam on equal terms," she said.

"What do you mean?" I asked.

"It was easy," she said. "I explained to Dr. James about the competition. And he agreed to remove your cast two days early."

They might drive you crazy. But sometimes parents can be your strongest allies!

Chapter 6

Friends

Beth and I had become friends. What's more, her mother offered to make my costumes! She said she loved sewing.

Beth and I worked hard to get ready for the competition. She had improved a lot. Our trio was actually getting quite good. But Pam seemed to try to mess it up when we danced in class.

"The judge watches your eyes," I told Beth. "So don't look sideways at me. Look straight ahead. Now—hands flexed and feet pointed and strong. *One* and *two* and . . ."

One Saturday, Beth and I were exercising at my house. As dancers, we knew the importance of strength and fitness.

Tony came in, flopped down, and began to eat some chips. I said, "Some people don't care about fitness."

"I get fit in the summer when I run," said Tony. "Anyway, what would you wimpy dancers know about fitness?"

So I told him that dancers need great strength and muscle control. And that *they* eat healthy food.

When Mom heard us, she said, "OK, we'll see who's fittest." She stood with her back to the wall. Then she gently slid down until her thighs were even with the floor. She looked as if she was sitting on a chair. "See how long you can do this," she said.

Owen fell down giggling after ten seconds. Beth lasted half a minute. The strain on my thigh muscles was awful, but I focused hard. A minute later, Tony groaned and slid to the floor. I stood up slowly when I was ready. Then I lazily bent over backward until my fingers touched the floor behind me. "Goodness me. I could have stayed there for twice as long," I smiled.

"Fitness freak!" grunted Tony.

But after that, I noticed that he didn't tease me about my dancing.

Chapter 7

Victory

I thought that Rick had accepted my dancing, too. But the day before the competition, he realized that Mom was driving me to all of my classes.

"This running around stops—today! You need to get your rest," he said to Mom.

"So how is Mel going to get to town for the competition tomorrow?" Mom replied.

"She can take a bus, of course."

"No way!" I broke in angrily. "Can you see me on a bus, loaded down with all of my costumes?" I stormed off to my room.

When I calmed down, I crept out and phoned Beth. "What am I going to do?" I wailed. Of course, she fixed the problem in no time. Her mom would come and get me.

I was nearly sick with excitement the next morning. Beth was just plain nervous. "Don't forget to look as if you're enjoying it," I reminded her. "Smiles earn lots of points."

At the end of the day, I had *five* firsts and *two* seconds! Even our trio got a third place.

Beth got a medal as the best beginner in our age group. She was wild with excitement.

I waited anxiously to find out how Pam had done. Finally she came up to me with a smug look. "I got *three* firsts, *two* seconds, and a third," she announced.

"What a shame, Pam," I replied. "I got *two* more firsts than you."

Chapter 8

Ignoring
the
Enemy

"Don't think that's the end of it," Pam said to me the next week. She had just watched me practice the solo section of the finale. That, of course, was my reward for winning. What was she going to do? Push me off the stage? I ignored her.

In the month before the recital, we worked hard at improving our dancing. At each lesson, we heard nothing but "Your hands are not strong enough. The fingers point down at this stage. Everyone, we have to straighten out those arms." Or "That footwork is messy!" Boring? No—I loved every minute of it.

My wrist was not strong yet. So the last dance started with me on stage alone. Then the rest of the class cartwheeled in to join me.

My solo followed. Pam annoyed me by copying my steps in the background at each practice. But I was really happy, and I just ignored her.

Rick and Mom decided that the whole family would go to Tony's football awards. They would also go to Owen's class play *and* my recital. Now they would all see why I loved jazz so much. I breezed through the last week smiling. What could go wrong now?

Chapter 9

Finale

The younger dancers were really excited. They were running everywhere when I got to the hall. Somehow I found Beth in the crowd. Pam was keeping her distance from the two of us.

I lined up to get my makeup on. That was so cool. You really feel like another person in a costume and makeup. I just grinned when Matthew told me that I looked great.

I'll never know what made me go and check my other costumes. Perhaps it was the smug look on Pam's face.

I went back to where I had hung up my costumes before I went to get my makeup done. One, two, three, four—I started to search in a panic.

"What's the matter, Mel?" asked Miss Narelle.

I felt sick. "My gold costume for the finale is missing!" I wailed.

She snapped, "You should have been more careful. I told you all to check the racks yesterday." Then she added, "Well, you can't do your solo without it."

Pam came forward. "My silver dress would be just perfect, and I know the dance well," she said. "Perhaps I should change places with Mel?"

I was speechless. It was so clear! But to my horror, Miss Narelle agreed. Nothing must spoil *her* recital.

Beth found me huddled in a corner. I told her what had happened. A strange look came over her face. "Come out here," she said, pointing at the back door.

She headed straight for the dumpster and hauled out a shopping bag.

"Beth, you'll get dirty," I warned. What *was* she doing? Then she fished out my costume!

"Pam did it," she said. "We got here early. So we stayed in our car for about five minutes. And I saw Pam run out. She stuffed this bag into the dumpster!"

There was just enough time to fix things up. Miss Narelle told Pam off. Then Pam said that she wasn't staying for the stupid recital. But Miss Narelle made her. "Dancers *never* let the troupe down," she said. "Now, get in line, all of you."

The end of my solo, with all of the other dancers on stage, was the best moment of my life. We stood quite still, hands raised. Then golden balloons drifted down onto us. The audience exploded with applause. Even Tony!

I suppose you think that this story should end with Pam saying she was sorry. And with me accepting her apology.

NO WAY! We still can't stand the sight of each other!

About the Author

Elizabeth Hutchins

Elizabeth Hutchins's dancing career began and ended when she was four years old and had a role in *The Water Babies.*

Elizabeth's talent went unnoticed because when a decoration on her costume began to fall off, she became so focused on reattaching it that she stood in the center of the stage—not moving so much as a toe. She still remembers the applause when her teacher finally picked her up and removed her to the wings!

Wanting to revisit that excitement, she decided to learn about jazz ballet for this book. To do this, she talked to teachers and students at two ballet schools and enjoyed their performances.

About the Illustrator

Michelle Ker

Michelle Ker lives in a big, old, rambling house with a dog, a cat, and some nosy neighbors who think that she is odd and wonder what she does all day in that room under the house.

Michelle loves music and plays drums. She gets a lot of the ideas for how characters look from watching rock bands.

She does all kinds of drawings for all kinds of people, but she likes drawing for kids' books the best. The characters have more fun, do mischievous things, and have better hairdos than people in other kinds of books.